Itch Scritch Scratch

To Andrew, Catherine and Flora

Published in 2013 in Great Britain by
Barrington Stoke Ltd
18 Walker Street, Edinburgh, EH3 7LP

www.barringtonstoke.co.uk

Reprinted 2017, 2018

This story was first published in a different form in
Wow! 366, Scholastic Children's Books, 2008

Text © 2008 Eleanor Updale
Illustrations © 2013 Sarah Horne

A CIP catalogue record for this book is available
from the British Library upon request

Individual ISBN: 978-1-78112-298-3
Pack ISBN: 978-1-78112-308-9

Not available separately

Printed in China by Leo

Barrington Stoke

ELEANOR UPDALE

Illustrated by Sarah Horne

Itch Scritch Scratch

I have a lot of little friends,

Who live upon my head.

They jog and jive and jiggle

When I am in my bed.

And then, when I am fast asleep,

Their wives start laying eggs.

Each egg contains a little louse,

With lots of little legs.

5

I saw one down a microscope,

His body looked like jelly.

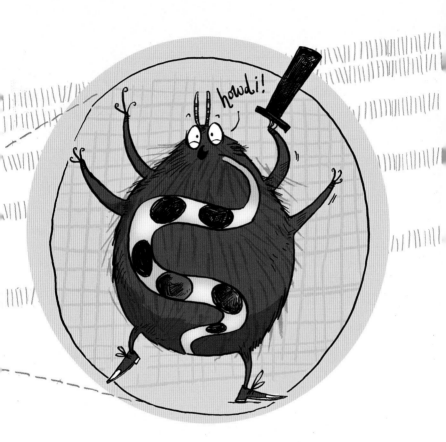

I could even see his poo

Working through his belly.

He had six legs with evil claws

To cling onto my hair,

And two short pointy aerials

That he waved in the air.

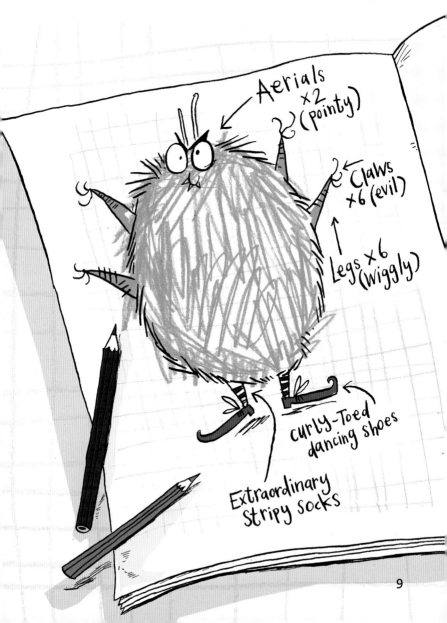

Lice don't make any honey,

They don't spin any thread,

You can't sell them for money,

You can't eat them with bread.

To my mind, lice are useless,

And it's worse than you expected,

They make you itch, they make you scratch,

Those bites can get infected!

13

My mum went mad with chemicals,

With shampoo and a comb,

Till yells and screams of agony

Rang from our happy home.

My sister, who has longer hair,

Could only scream and shout

As my mum brushed and combed and tugged,

To get the head lice out.

17

But all their eggs were stuck with glue

Extruded from their tummies.

My mum tried everything she could,

And so did other mummies.

They cursed, they swore, they hoovered us

To get the lice away,

Weee!

But those bugs just kept on laying eggs,

To hatch another day.

21

Each lady louse lays 83,

And each of them lays more.

There really is no way that we

Can hope to win this war.

YIP
YIP!

But it's not all bad. Just think of this –

In one way they're quite cool.

'Cause if you show the teachers them,

You get the day off school.

NOW PLEASE STOP SCRATCHING!

Are you NUTS about stories?

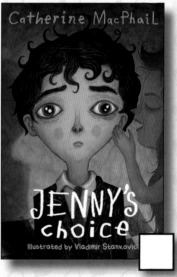

Read ALL the Acorns!